# Look What I Can Do!

BY Nancy Viau

Illustrated BY Anna Vojtech

Abrams Books for Young Readers
New York

For my mother, who
made everything look easy
— NV

To my family, and all
families everywhere
— AV

Library of Congress Cataloging-in-Publication Data

Viau, Nancy.
Look what I can do! / by Nancy Viau ; illustrated by Anna Vojtech.
p. cm.
Summary: Baby animals overcome challenges in their day-to-day lives, such as finding food,
spinning a web, and flying from the nest.
ISBN 978-1-4197-0529-8
[1. Stories in rhyme. 2. Animals—Infancy—Fiction. 3. Growth—Fiction.]
I. Vojtech, Anna, ill. II. Title.
PZ8.3.V712667Lo 2013
[E]—dc23
2012018807

Printed and bound in China
10 9 8 7 6 5 4 3 2 1

Abrams Books for Young Readers are available at special discounts when purchased in quantity for premiums
and promotions as well as fundraising or educational use. Special editions can also be created to specification.
For details, contact specialsales@abramsbooks.com or the address below.

ABRAMS
THE ART OF BOOKS SINCE 1949
115 West 18th Street
New York, NY 10011
www.abramsbooks.com

*I*t's not easy to stand up strong.
I shake and sway, but move along.

It's not easy to slither fast.
I slide downhill. I won't be last.

*I*t's not easy to catch a fly.
I flick my tongue.
I leap so high.

riends of forest, field, and stream,
   Keep trying on your own.
Be proud today.
Have fun and play.
In time you will be grown.

It's not easy to leave the nest.
I flap my wings. I try my best.

It's not easy to spin a trap.
I need a snack. I need a nap.

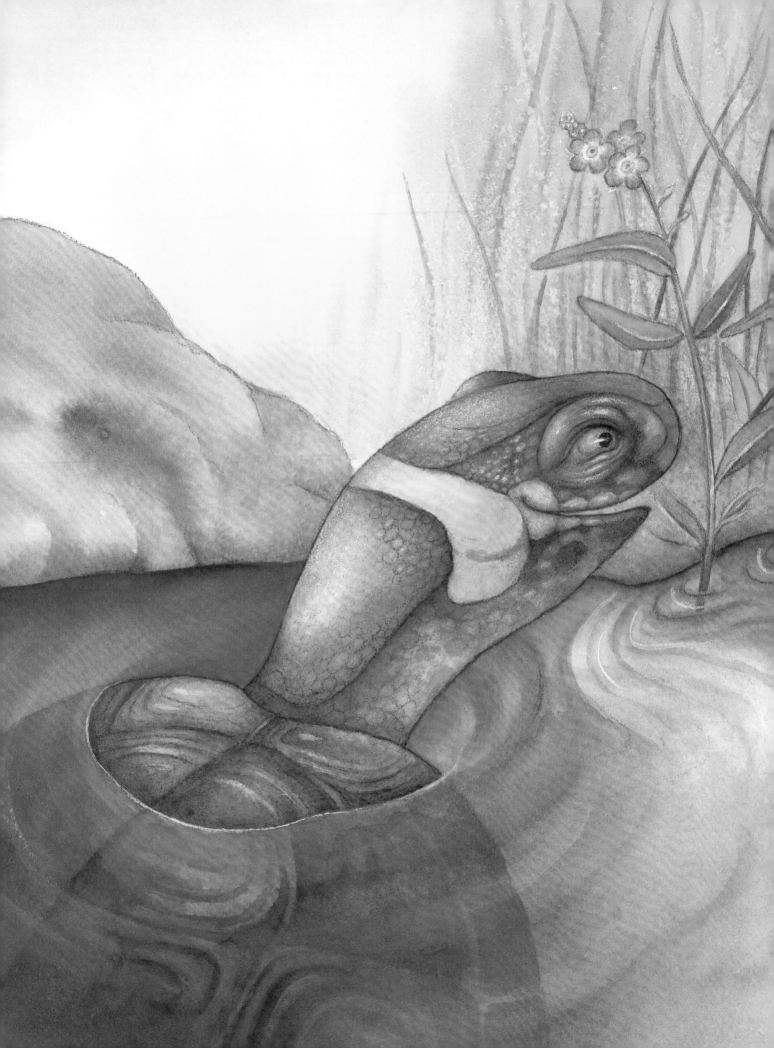

It's not easy to cross the path.
My feet are tired. I want a bath.

$\mathcal{F}$riends of forest,
field, and stream,
Keep trying on your own.
Be proud today.
Have fun and play.
In time you will be grown.

It's not easy to find my place.
I hide a nut, but leave a trace.

It's not easy to reach the twig.
I stretch up tall. Hey look, I'm big!

*I*t's not easy to fish each day.
I swipe my paw. He swims away.

Friends of forest,
field, and stream,
Keep trying on your own.
Be proud today.
Have fun and play.
In time you will be grown.

It's not easy to step, then hop.
Skip one, skip two. I'll never stop!

It's not easy to hit a ball.
But I can catch it as it falls.